Dear Parents and Educators,

Welcome to Penguin Young Readers! As parents and educators, you know that each child develops at his or her own pace—in terms of speech, critical thinking, and, of course, reading. Penguin Young Readers recognizes this fact. As a result, each Penguin Young Readers book is assigned a traditional easy-to-read level (1–4) as well as a Guided Reading Level (A–P). Both of these systems will help you choose the right book for your child. Please refer to the back of each book for specific leveling information. Penguin Young Readers features esteemed authors and illustrators, stories about favorite characters, fascinating nonfiction, and more!

On a Farm

This book is perfect for an **Emergent Reader** who:

- can read in a left-to-right and top-to-bottom progression;
- can recognize some beginning and ending letter sounds;
- can use picture clues to help tell the story; and
- can understand the basic plot and sequence of simple stories.

Here are some **activities** you can do during and after reading this book:

- Picture Clues: In this book, the pictures can help the child read the words. Reread the story and point to the words and the corresponding pictures. Then write the words on sticky paper and place them on the pictures. For example, write the word *cherries* and place it on the picture of the cherries.
- Patterns: This book uses several sentence patterns, such as "_____ live on a farm." Reread the story and point out the different patterns to the child. Then, on a separate sheet of paper, use each sentence pattern to write a new sentence. For example, "Goats live on a farm."

Remember, sharing the love of reading with a child is the best gift you can give!

—Bonnie Bader, EdM
Penguin Young Readers program

*Penguin Young Readers are leveled by independent reviewers applying the standards developed by Irene Fountas and Gay Su Pinnell in *Matching Books to Readers: Using Leveled Books in Guided Reading*, Heinemann, 1999.

To my grandma Jeanne, who taught me everything I needed to know to grow a beautiful garden. I love you—CK

Penguin Young Readers
Published by the Penguin Group
Penguin Group (USA) Inc., 375 Hudson Street, New York, New York 10014, USA
Penguin Group (Canada), 90 Eglinton Avenue East, Suite 700, Toronto, Ontario M4P 2Y3, Canada
(a division of Pearson Penguin Canada Inc.)
Penguin Books Ltd, 80 Strand, London WC2R 0RL, England
Penguin Ireland, 25 St Stephen's Green, Dublin 2, Ireland (a division of Penguin Books Ltd)
Penguin Group (Australia), 707 Collins Street, Melbourne, Victoria 3008, Australia
(a division of Pearson Australia Group Pty Ltd)
Penguin Books India Pvt Ltd, 11 Community Centre, Panchsheel Park, New Delhi—110 017, India
Penguin Group (NZ), 67 Apollo Drive, Rosedale, Auckland 0632, New Zealand
(a division of Pearson New Zealand Ltd)
Penguin Books, Rosebank Office Park, 181 Jan Smuts Avenue, Parktown North 2193, South Africa
Penguin China, B7 Jaiming Center, 27 East Third Ring Road North,
Chaoyang District, Beijing 100020, China

Penguin Books Ltd, Registered Offices: 80 Strand, London WC2R 0RL, England

Photo credits: cover: (chick, tractor) © iStockphoto/Thinkstock; cover, page 3: (apples) © iStockphoto/Thinkstock, (pig) © Hemera/Thinkstock; page 5: © iStockphoto/Thinkstock; page 6: © iStockphoto/Thinkstock; page 7: (barn) © iStockphoto/Thinkstock, (cow, calf) © Hemera/Thinkstock; page 8: © iStockphoto/Thinkstock; page 9: © iStockphoto/Thinkstock; page 10: © iStockphoto/Thinkstock; page 11: (barn) © iStockphoto/Thinkstock, (goat, kid) © Hemera/Thinkstock; page 12: © iStockphoto/Thinkstock; page 13: © iStockphoto/Thinkstock; page 15: © iStockphoto/Thinkstock; page 16: © iStockphoto/Thinkstock; page 17: © iStockphoto/Thinkstock; page 18: © iStockphoto/Thinkstock; page 19: © iStockphoto/Thinkstock; page 20: © iStockphoto/Thinkstock; page 21: (barn, potato pile) © iStockphoto/Thinkstock, (single potato) © Hemera/Thinkstock; page 22: © iStockphoto/Thinkstock; page 23: © iStockphoto/Thinkstock; page 25: © iStockphoto/Thinkstock; page 26: © iStockphoto/Thinkstock; page 27: © iStockphoto/Thinkstock; page 28: (barn) © iStockphoto/Thinkstock, (wheelbarrow) © Stockbyte/Thinkstock; page 29: © iStockphoto/Thinkstock; page 30: (barn) © iStockphoto/Thinkstock, (truck) © Hemera/Thinkstock; page 31: © iStockphoto/Thinkstock; page 32: © iStockphoto/Thinkstock.

Published by Penguin Young Readers, an imprint of Penguin Group (USA) Inc.,
345 Hudson Street, New York, New York 10014. Manufactured in China.

Library of Congress Cataloging-in-Publication Data is available.

ISBN 978-0-448-46376-6 (pbk) 10 9 8 7 6 5 4 3 2 1
ISBN 978-0-448-46505-0 (hc) 10 9 8 7 6 5 4 3 2 1

On a Farm

by Alexa Andrews
illustrated by Candice Keimig
and with photographs

Penguin Young Readers
An Imprint of Penguin Group (USA) Inc.

Animals

Horses live on a farm.

Cows live on a farm.

Sheep live on a farm.

Chickens live on a farm.

Turkeys live on a farm.

Goats live on a farm.

Pigs live on a farm.

Dogs live on a farm.

Food

Apples grow on a farm.

Pears grow on a farm.

Cherries grow on a farm.

Carrots grow on a farm.

Tomatoes grow on a farm.

Potatoes grow on a farm.

Pumpkins grow on a farm.

Corn grows on a farm.

On a Farm

Hay is on a farm.

A tractor is on a farm.

A wheelbarrow is on a farm.

A rake is on a farm.

A truck is on a farm.

A scarecrow is on a farm.

A barn is on a farm.